MORE
NANNY AND GRANDAD
ADVENTURES

- NANNY AND GRANDAD GO INTO SPACE
- NANNY AND GRANDAD SPEND THE DAY ON THE RIVER
- NANNY AND GRANDAD HAVE VISITORS IN THE NIGHT

Copyright 2021 by Martin Harman

Published by Harman Books

ISBN: 978-1-9163978-2-8

Illustrations by Raynald Kudemus

Creative and Print by SpiffingCovers.com

NANNY AND GRANDAD AND THE PIRATES OF DEVON

MARTIN HARMAN

HARMAN

BOOKS

FOR
FINLEY, LILY, SUSIE AND JESSE

EACH ONE OF YOU ARE THE
TREASURE IN MY LIFE

It was a lovely day. Nanny and Grandad were sitting on a couple of deck chairs next to their caravan overlooking the sea. The sun was shining and they had just had a nice cup of tea. Nanny was doing a crossword puzzle and Grandad had been reading a book about pirates in Devon.

He put his book down on the grass and took in the view. The sea was calm and the sun was shimmering on the sea with hardly a cloud in the sky and only a soft breeze in the air.

Behind him the village clock struck 11 O'clock and the ravens were squawking in the distance mixed with the sound of seagulls flying overhead.

"What a lovely day" said Grandad to Nanny, "the world is at peace and we are so lucky to be enjoying such a warm summer."

Nanny looked up and took in the lovely view. "Look out there" she said, "look at that large sailing boat with the red sails. It's often sailing across the bay. I wonder what they do and where they go every day? They always seem to be going somewhere."

"Mmm" said Grandad, "I bet they're up to no good."

"What are you talking about?" asked Nanny, "they're just sailing about the bay, minding their own business, how could they be up to no good?"

Grandad wasn't so sure, he picked up his book and carried on reading about the Devon pirates and how, many years ago they had sailed these seas. They had been smugglers as well as pirates, attacking merchant ships and stealing their cargo. That had been a long time ago.

Of course there were no pirates around Devon now or at least not that anyone knew about. As Grandad looked up from his book, he looked again at the boat with the red sails and wondered what their business was.

"Come on" said Nanny, "let's not sit here all day, we'll catch the bus into Dartmouth and go to that nice tea shop. Then have a walk along the river front."

"Now that does sound like a good idea" said Grandad, "I wonder if they have any lemon drizzle cake."

Quickly they cleared up their cups, put their deck chairs away, changed their clothes and walked to the bus stop opposite the caravan site where they waited for the late morning bus that would take them into town in time for lunch.

The bus was on time, they paid the driver for a return fare for two and took a seat at the front of the bus on the top deck. As the bus approached Dartmouth through the country lanes, they caught glimpses of the sea and river.

"Look" said Grandad, "there's that boat with the red sails, it looks like it's heading into the harbour."

As the bus pulled into Dartmouth, the boat was just coming past the castle that guards the town. It pulled up at the bus stop and everyone got off .

"Shall we see where the boat is going to stop?" asked Grandad.

"No" said Nanny "let's go and have lunch, stop worrying about that boat."

"Oh, ok but I would like to know what they are up to."

Nanny and Grandad stopped at the little teashop near the harbour and ordered jam & cucumber sandwiches, tea for two and a big slice of lemon drizzle cake each.

The noise of the wheel smashing made the pirates look back and shout, "Hey! Who are you and what are you doing on board our boat? What have you done to our steering wheel?"

Grandad jumped into the little boat next to Nanny and tried to untie the rope but he was struggling with the knot.

The big pirate was now running along the deck towards them with the other pirates right behind him.

"Hurry up!" said Nanny,

"I can't undo the knot" said Grandad,

"Out of the way" said Nanny, "let me have a look at it."

Just then the big pirate grabbed the other end of the rope. "Who are you?" he shouted, "What are you doing on my boat?"

He started to pull the little boat towards him just as Nanny finally undid the knot and the little boat slipped away.

Just then the big pirate looked over his shoulder as the other pirates started to shout something to him. Nanny and Grandad paddled with their hands towards the riverbank and safety.

"Hurry up" said Nanny, "the pirates will soon be able to catch us once they turn their boat around."

"Don't worry about that," said Grandad, "I smashed their steering wheel so they can't steer the boat, and look..." Grandad pointed at the pirate's boat.

Nanny looked as the pirate's boat was heading towards the rocks under the castle. The pirates on board were rushing around trying to slow the boat and stop it from crashing into the rocks.

Nanny and Grandad just reached the shore when there was a terrible crashing noise. They both scrambled ashore and looked at the pirate's boat as it hit the rocks and the main mast came tumbling down and crashed onto the deck of the boat.

As Nanny and Grandad stood on the shore and watched the pirate's boat, they could see the pirates scramble onto the rocks.

"Well" said Grandad, "that put an end to their little game, should we call the Police?"

"Come on" said Nanny, "I think we have done enough damage for one day and we don't want to get any more involved than we have already been." She looked at her watch. "We still have time to catch the bus home if we hurry."

Grandad opened a door at the end of the cabin and went into the next room. Hanging on the wall in the cabin were a number of large maps of the coast of Devon with marks showing boats with crosses next to them.

"Look at those maps" said Grandad, "those crosses must be the boats that they have attacked in the bay, I told you they were pirates."

"You're letting your imagination run away with you again," said Nanny.

"Now stop being silly and let's get off this boat and look for the right one that will take us for a trip around the bay. I am not interested in your silly ideas about pirates. I just want to have a nice peaceful afternoon without any excitement."

Just then they heard loud voices and a couple of thumps as someone jumped on board the boat. "Hand me those supplies," said a loud voice from above, "look lively there, we have to be quick if we're to get everything ready before the tide goes out."

"See!" said Grandad, "I told you they were up to no good, it sounds like they're going to attack another ship."

"Oh my goodness" said Nanny anxiously "now what are we going to do?"

"Quick!" said Grandad, "let's go through that door, maybe it leads back on deck and we can jump onto the jetty."

Grandad opened the door but it didn't lead anywhere. It was a small storeroom. They had no time to try the other door on the other side of the cabin so they both squeezed through the door and into the small room.

"Quick shut the door," said Nanny.

Just before one of the men came all the way down the steps into the cabin Nanny and Grandad shut the storeroom door but could still see a little of the cabin through a small gap at the edge of the door and could see a big man in the cabin.

"Get those supplies stored and let's get underway," said the big man.

"How many of them are there?" whispered Nanny,

"Not sure" said Grandad, "but I think there may be about four of them."

"What do we do now?" asked Nanny.

Before Grandad could answer, the boat engine started and a voice shouted...

"CAST OFF, FORE!, CAST OFF, AFT!"

"Oh my goodness, what have you got us into this time?" said Nanny, looking very annoyed.

"I'm sorry, I didn't *really* think they were pirates," said Grandad, "I just got a little carried away after reading my book. Whoever thought we had pirates here in Devon, in this age?"

"Well we are certainly getting carried away now," said Nanny, "they do sound like pirates and they're going to attack another boat, with us caught up in the middle."

The boat started to roll as it moved away from the jetty and head for the castle and the open sea.

"Quick as you like" shouted the big man, "we need to be in position before night so we can come around the point just before 8 o'clock. We have to come up on the sea-side so we keep off the rocks."

Nanny was looking through the crack in the door and saw the big man go back up the steps and close the cabin door behind him.

"He's left the cabin and gone up on deck" whispered Nanny, "what shall we do? We can't just stay here, they may catch us. You have to think of something to get us out of this mess."

"I told you" said Grandad, "I've read about them in my book. They board ships just before night time while the crews are having dinner and they capture the ships, take the cargo and make the crew walk the plank."

MIKE HUNT

SMELLS LIKE FISH

"Oh dear" said Nanny, quite concerned now. "I really don't fancy walking the plank, I have my best hat on and the sea water will ruin my hair."

Grandad looked about the cabin to see if there was any way they could escape. Looking out the small window he could see they were still sailing down the river and had not yet sailed out to sea. He looked up and saw a hatch in the cabin ceiling.

"Quick!" said Grandad, "help me move the table so I can climb up and lift the hatch to see if we can get out."

They moved the table under the hatch. Grandad climbed onto the table and gently lifted the hatch. He lifted it an inch and looked out. He could see four pirates at the other end of the boat. It looked like they were sorting through the boxes of supplies they had brought on board.

As Grandad looked around the deck, the end of a rope kept flapping against the hatch. He grabbed it to stop it making a noise and wondered what it was tied to. He quietly lifted the hatch a little more and looked up to see it was connected to the big front sail. He grabbed the rope with both hands and pulled but nothing moved. It was tied tight.

Just then another boat went past and the wash from it made a wave that made the pirate's boat rock.

Grandad was sent off balance, he slipped on the table but he hung onto the rope. The rope held for a split second and then gave way. Grandad fell all the way to the floor, right on top of Nanny, but he still held the end of the rope that had now come loose.

CRASH!

There was a crashing sound from above and something heavy fell on top of the hatch, banging it shut.

The pirate's boat now started to lose speed and there was lots of shouting and running on the deck.

"Oh, what have you done?" said Nanny. "And will you get off me!"

"I'm not sure what I've done," said Grandad, "but I think I have made one of the sails crash to the deck and it sounded like the mast also snapped. The sail must have flapped free when I pulled the rope and somehow that broke the mast."

This time Nanny climbed up on to the table to look out from under the hatch but it would only open an inch because the sail had landed on it. This blocked their way out but Nanny could just see enough to spot where the pirates were.

"Quick" said Nanny, "all the pirates are at the front of the boat trying to sort the sail out, so we may be able to get on deck and look for a way to get off the boat."

Grandad helped Nanny off the table and they both rushed through the cabin and up the stairs. They looked out of the cabin door to check where the pirates were.

"Yes" she said, "look they are all still at the other end of the boat."

They both climbed up on deck and looked for a way to get off the boat. The pirates were all busy trying to untangle the sail, so didn't notice Nanny and Grandad come out of the cabin door.

"Look" said Nanny and pointed to the very back of the boat.

Tied to the back of the pirate's sailing boat was a little wooden dinghy.

"Come on" said Grandad. "If we're quick we can get into that dinghy before they notice us."

Grandad held Nanny's hand and they ran down the length of the boat to the back, where the dinghy was tied to the railing.

Grandad grabbed the rope tied to the dinghy and pulled the dinghy close to the pirate's boat.

"In you get" said Grandad, as he helped Nanny over the side of the boat and into the little dinghy.

Nanny looked up to Grandad and said "If the pirates see us they will steer their boat around and catch us. We need one of your cunning plans."

Grandad looked around and saw a heavy looking box. It was one of the boxes the pirates had brought on board. He picked it up and smashed it against the boat's steering wheel, breaking the wheel into pieces.

After lunch they went for a walk along the harbour. There was always some activity on the river. They found a seat in the sun and watched the boats come and go.

"Look at that poster over by the jetty" said Nanny, "it looks like there are boat rides around the bay, how do you fancy a boat trip? It's such a lovely day."

"Sounds good to me" said Grandad.

So up they got and walked down to the jetty to look for the boat taking holidaymakers around the bay. At the end of the jetty was the boat with the red sails.

"That must be the boat" said Grandad, "let's get on board."

"I don't think that is the boat taking people on trips around the bay" said Nanny, "I have never seen a sailing boat give pleasure cruises."

"Let's just have a look," said Grandad.

They got to the boat but it looked deserted.

"Hello!" called Grandad, "Anybody there?"

"Let's leave," said Nanny, "I'm sure this isn't the right boat."

"Hang on" said Grandad, "we're here now, let's have a look on board, maybe everyone is below deck."

"No!" said Nanny, "I'm telling you this is not the boat!"

There was no stopping Grandad, quick as a flash he climbed up the steps and was standing on the deck before Nanny had a chance to stop him.

"Get off that boat!" demanded Nanny "before anyone sees you."

"Don't be silly," said Grandad, "we might as well have a look around now we're here. I'm sure this is the right boat, I can't see any other boat on the jetty. Come on give me your hand."

Reluctantly Nanny held Grandad's hand as he helped her onto the deck.

"I'm not sure about this" said Nanny anxiously, "I don't like it, let's go."

"Let's just have a look below deck to see if the Captain is there" said Grandad as he opened the door to the main cabin and went below with Nanny close behind him.

It was a lot bigger than it looked from the outside. They were standing in the main cabin with a couple of doors leading off to other cabins and cupboards.

"I told you this was the wrong boat!" said Nanny, "now let's go before anyone sees us."

"Hang on" said Grandad, "let's see if we can find any clues as to why they're always sailing around the bay. If they're not giving people rides, maybe they are pirates like in the book I have been reading."

"Don't be silly" said Nanny, "you don't get pirates in Devon."

They hurried back along the shore path into town, keeping an eye on the road behind them in case any of the pirates had seen where they landed and came after them. As they got to the bus stop they were just in time to catch the last bus home to their caravan.

The bus stopped outside their caravan site and off they got, thanking the bus driver. As they were walking away from the bus Nanny said, "Well that was scary, but you did a good job Grandad in causing their boat to crash. Maybe the ships along the coast will be safe now. Well done, you have stopped the Pirates of Devon."

Grandad felt very proud of himself. "Yes" he said, puffing his chest out, "I did do a good job, maybe the town Mayor will give me a medal."

When they finally got back home to their caravan Nanny put the kettle on to make a cup of tea for them both while Grandad turned the telly on to watch the evening news.

Nanny made them both a cup of tea and opened a new packet of biscuits. Grandad picked up a biscuit and dipped it into his tea and as they both watched the news. Right before them on the telly was a picture of the pirate's boat wrecked on the rocks under Dartmouth Castle. Grandad had a big smile on his face and his chest pumped out in pride. "Thought they could get the better of Grandad did they?" he smiled.

"Turn the sound up," said Nanny.

Grandad turned the telly up and they both stopped and stared as the newsreader announced...

" A small 'supply' boat has crashed onto the rocks near the castle at Dartmouth and supplies meant for the lighthouse have all been lost in the river. The crew have reported that an old man and woman had been seen on board the boat and had caused it to crash. "

"Oh no!" said Nanny, "they weren't pirates at all, but just sailors delivering supplies to the lighthouse."

She looked at Grandad who was now looking a little sheepish. "What have you done?" scowled Nanny. "You, and your book about pirates, and you thought you were going to get a medal? I'm not sure a medal is what the Mayor will be thinking right now. What am I going to do with you?"

Grandad stared open mouthed at the telly and said, "I don't understand, I thought they were pirates," as his soggy biscuit fell into his tea.

For more

ADVENTURES OF
NANNY AND GRANDAD

Visit: HarmanBooks.com

Printed in Great Britain
by Amazon